Redeeming Fire

By:
Leah Pugh

Copyright © 2024 Leah Pugh

All rights reserved. This work of fiction is protected under International and Federal Copyright Laws and Treaties. Any unauthorized reprint or use of this material is prohibited. No part of this book may be reproduced or transmitted in any form or by any means, electronic or mechanical, including photocopying, recording, or by any information storage and retrieval system without express written permission from the author, Leah Pugh, except where permitted by law.

The characters and events portrayed in this book are fictitious. Names, characters, places, and incidents are the product of the author's imagination. Any resemblance to actual persons, living or dead, business establishments, events, or locales is entirely coincidental.

Dedication

This story is dedicated to the firefighters, EMTs, and police officers, who put their lives on the line for the safety of others. Thank you.

Acknowledgments

Thank you to the firefighters, police officer, and retired arson investigator who reviewed this story and offered the necessary feedback.

To my critique group, thank you for being patient with me and reading this piece over and over. You all rock!

"Unit 1David26, Dispatch." I parked down the road from the thick cloud of smoke pouring out of the residence in the middle of the street. "Roll fire and rescue to the 1200 block of Murphy Street. Residence fire fully involved. I'll be out checking!"

"Fire and Rescue are three to five minutes out," Dispatch responded.

"10 – 4."

I activated my body camera and approached the spectators gathering on the sidewalk and near the house.

"Thank God you're here!" a woman wearing a jogging suit cried. "Everyone's out…at least I think they are."

As I quickly assessed the situation, a small crowd of people on the front lawn and smoke pouring out of the two-story farmhouse, my mind suddenly wandered down a dark path to a place I fought desperately to stay away from.

Against my will, my mind put me back in my old living room. I could feel the heat brushing across my face as the acrid, stinging smell of burning polyurethane furniture and plastic seared my nostrils.

"Jay! Jay, help me!" Emily's screams vibrated through my soul.

"I'm coming! Hang on!" I tried to sound hopeful, even though I could barely see my hand in front of my face.

Smoke swirled around me, causing me to lose my bearings and trip over the coffee table. And then nothing.

"Oh no! I don't think she's out here!" Jogging Suit Lady's frantic scream jarred me back to reality.

"Who?" I demanded.

Before she could respond, a petite, middle-aged woman broke away from the crowd and barreled for the house. A man, at least a head taller, overtook her in a few strides and tried pulling her back. She fought him like a cat about to get fixed.

"What's going on here?" I rushed over.

"She's in there!" the woman screamed. "I've got to save my baby!"

"Ma'am, who?"

"Our six-year-old daughter, Nadalia," the man said.

My heart sank into the pit of my stomach. *Oh no, not a child trapped inside.*

The couple started arguing, their words overlapping each other unintelligibly. I heard bits and pieces of it.

"Jeffrey, I was in the kitchen when you yelled for us to get out and I thought she was right behind me when I went out the back door! Didn't you see her, too?"

"I was coughing so hard, I could barely see where I was going, and even tripped over the busted chair on my way out, Alicia. I thought she was behind *me* when I went out the front door."

The crowd didn't help, adding their own shouts and comments.

"Everyone needs to stay calm." Despite my unruffled, authoritative voice, I felt anything but as the rest of that awful memory played out.

When I finally came back into the world of reality after tripping over the coffee table, I was told the hideous truth. My beloved wife and daughter, Emily and Angie, were no more, having died of smoke inhalation from a fire that started because Emily had forgotten to turn the gas stove off and left a pot on the same burner.

The smoke detector hadn't gone off because the batteries were dead. I always worked four ten-hour shifts and was 'too busy' to fix the detector. Guilt became my constant companion ever since that day. Hounding me almost every waking moment.

If only I'd gone to see that sleep specialist like Emily wanted me to, she wouldn't have kicked me to the couch for snoring so loud, I thought. *If only I hadn't slacked in getting a new smoke detector. If only I hadn't gotten so disoriented in the smoke. If only I'd saved them. How Emily must hate me for not getting to her and Angie in time.*

Out of habit, I reached up and fingered the left side of my neck where the skin had been burnt off, and I'd had laser surgery to fix it.

Too bad the laser couldn't go deep enough to fix my scarred heart.

"Can't you do anything, Officer Jay?" the mom's cry brought me back to reality. "Please!"

"The fire department will be here soon, and they'll have everything under control." I could hear the sirens wailing ever so faintly in the distance. But as I looked back at the burning house, I didn't hold much hope for the fire department getting here in time to rescue their daughter.

Flames pointed their jagged fingers up at the heavens from open windows on the top floor, and smoke poured out as if a dragon were inside. There was no way I was going in there.

You've got to go in there, my conscience argued. *You swore an oath to serve and protect.*

I can't fail again, I argued back. *What if I make another mistake and another life is lost?*

But what if you go and a life is saved?

A flash of bright blue against the whitewashed color of the house made me look up. Little Angie stood on the top step wearing a matching bright sky-blue summer outfit, her light brown hair pulled up in pigtails, and she cradled her favorite stuffed bunny. It was her, and yet it wasn't. She was so thin and 2D, I could see right through her.

"Daddy!" she called. "Mommy says she's gonna kick your butt if you don't get up here right now!"

I blinked, and she vanished.

Great, now I'm imagining things! I decided to check on fire and rescue. "1David 26, ETA on fire? Parents believe they have a child trapped inside. Tell them to step it up!"

"1David 26, Fire and Rescue are held up by a train. Estimates are between five and seven minutes," was the disheartening response.

I'd totally forgotten about the three o'clock train.

"That's too long, Dispatch! Too long!" I barked into the mike, my frustration building. "Any other stations on the way?"

"Yes, but they're five to seven minutes away as well."

Jeffrey had relaxed his grip, and his wife took advantage of the fact. Without warning, she sprinted for the house.

"Alicia, no!" he cried.

I took after her and grabbed her arm before she could reach the bottom porch step.

"If you go barreling in there, the added oxygen will cause the house to explode!" I yelled.

She stopped struggling as tears of helplessness streamed down her face and we made eye contact. I did a double take. Emily's chocolate brown eyes stared back at me, silently pleading for help.

Is that how Emily's eyes actually looked in her final moments? Crying out for help that wasn't coming? I made a decision. "I'm heading in. Don't anyone go in there, or I'll cuff you and throw you in the back of my car, got it?"

Jeffrey gripped his wife's arm tightly. "Got it."

I tore for the squad car, removing my radio and gun belt as I ran, and popped the trunk. Placing the items in the trunk, I opted to leave the vest on for protection. For extra protection, I donned a jacket, a pair of Kevlar gloves, and a wool cap.

Grab the riot helmet, my brain suggested. *You never know.*

I donned the helmet and paused. For a split second, I thought I heard the fire truck's blaring horn getting closer and almost changed my mind. But didn't hear it again.

My imagination is in overdrive today! I ran for the door and tested the knob; not hot.

The next step was to open the door carefully. When I was sure the house wasn't going to blow, I finally got it open enough to slip inside and drop to my knees.

It felt like I was in some Sci-Fi movie. The inside of the doorway was a lethal black with a strange gray hue. Taking a deep breath, I tripod slid deeper into the monster's mouth. I remembered making fun of my firefighter brother-in-law when he showed it to me, calling it an over glorified clamp slide. Now I sent up a silent prayer of thanks that he showed it to me.

Smoke instantly engulfed me, making breathing difficult despite the helmet. The heat was searing, even with my added protection. My eyes watered, and I blinked furiously to clear the tears. Nadalia was in here somewhere. I had to find her; I just had to.

"Nadalia! Naaadaliaa!" I hollered as loudly as I could, even though the helmet muffled my voice a bit. *They said she might be in the kitchen, but where is that? Should've asked before I came barreling in here!* "Nad – whoa!"

Plaster and debris crashed from above, startling me. Coughing harshly, I lost my balance. I wiped the dust from my eyes in time to see jagged pieces of a broken chair right in front of me. I threw my weight to the left, but didn't clear it entirely. Something sharp cut a gash in my right thigh. The pain was blinding as I fumbled to find out what it was. A nail protruded from the upper thigh. Gritting my teeth, I wriggled it out and tossed it aside.

Just got my tetanus shot updated this morning. Talk about perfect timing.

Blood seeped down my leg from a cut, and I struggled to put my full weight on the lower half of my body. When I was finally able to, I resumed the search. As I entered a small room, the familiar feeling of guilt began to play with my mind like a cat plays with a mouse before eating it.

You won't find Nadalia, and you know it, it taunted me. *You know you're just reliving June 1st all over again!*

I clenched my hands into fists as fear smothered me worse than the smoke around me. It felt like someone had covered me with a woolen blanket. Despite the intense heat, a cold sweat broke out on my forehead, my hands became clammy, and a metallic taste filled my mouth. The walls started slowly moving forward, their flat sides threatening to squash me.

My mind worked frantically, trying to remember some of the things I'd learned in the many years of therapy to overcome moments like this. However, my brain refused to cooperate; all I could focus on was fear.

I can't do it! I envisioned myself crawling back outside in defeat, telling someone else to hurry inside and find the child. That is, if help had arrived by now.

By then, it will be too late, the voice told me. *She may be dead, and you'll be responsible for her death. How would that look on your police records?*

"Heck, what am I worried about? The fire'll probably kill me before that happens!" I laughed dryly.

Jeffrey and Alicia's pleas for help flashed across my mind. They were helpless, unable to do anything as their house burned with their daughter trapped inside. The urge to turn tail and run outside became unbearable.

"Dear God, give me strength!" I cried out.

Smoke made breathing almost impossible, and I knew I couldn't stay in here for much longer.

"Hi, Daddy!"

"Angie!"

Again, there stood my daughter, clutching that stuffed rabbit. I wanted to reach out and touch her, see if she was real, but I was too unnerved to do anything but stare.

She smiled at me. "Mommy wants to know if you're hungry and wanna sandwich."

"A sandwich, what?"

"Well, if you want one, you gotta go to the kitchen and tell her." Spinning on her heel, she bounded off.

I slid after her and poked my head around a corner. "Angie?"

A fiery burst of flame belched at me, and I jumped backward. Suddenly, a sound arrested my attention, sending chills racing up and down my spine. It sounded like a violin being played. I hadn't heard it in five years but knew that laugh anywhere. Gulping, I looked up and felt my eyes bug out. Standing ten feet in front of me was Emily. She wore a red shirt and ratty, cut-off jeans. Her chestnut hair was pulled back in a ponytail, and her brown eyes were laughing at me. She looked real, but at the same time faded, like an old photograph.

"Emily!" I called hoarsely.

"Sorry, but you always did look silly when something scared you. Now, did you tell Angie what sandwich you wanted?"

"Why is everyone going on about sandwiches? I'm trying to find a child and not only am I hallucinating, my hallucinations want to make me lunch!"

She frowned. "Well, Captain Picky, come to the kitchen and tell me what you want." Like Angie, Emily spun about on her heel and marched out of the room.

The kitchen, the kitchen...why does that sound so familiar? I wracked my brain. *Wait a minute, Alicia said that was the last place she saw Nadalia!*

"Hey, wait up!" I struggled to keep up with Emily, as pain sliced my leg every time blood pumped through it.

I managed to keep Emily's red shirt in sight and followed her through the smoky haze to what must have been the kitchen, judging by the sink and fridge. I entered the room just as she disappeared into a closet. The metal handle was practically glowing from the intense heat. It was now I dared get into a half standing, half crouching position, not standing up all the way because of the heat.

I knew better than to touch the handle, but I couldn't resist calling out, "Emily? Sweetie?"

The door swung open on its own accord. A little girl, no older than six, lay in a crumpled heap on the floor in front of me. Her limp, blond curls stuck to her face, and she loosely clutched a ratty teddy bear in her arms. It didn't look like her chest was moving.

"Nadalia!" *Dear God, no! Please don't let her be dead!* I had to get the child to safety! "Nadalia, if you can hear me, I'm going to take you outside."

There was still no movement as I hefted her up in my arms. In that instant, it wasn't Nadalia I was holding, but my baby girl, Angie. As I closed my eyes, I could feel Angie's soft eyelashes tickling my cheek as she gave me butterfly kisses. Her childish giggles made me smile, and Emily smiled back.

Falling ceiling plaster brought me back to the present, missing us by mere inches. I immediately dropped back to my knees, almost screaming in pain when my shins collided with the floor.

"Let's get out of…oh no!" I froze.

I didn't know which way to go! The smoke made everything look the same, gray and murky. Bits and pieces of the couples' argument came to mind.

"'Jeffrey, I was in the kitchen when you yelled for us to get out and I thought she was right behind me when I went out the back door!'"

"Where is the back door?!" Visibility was rapidly getting worse.

"Oh, Jay! You always were terrible at directions."

I was almost certain my blood froze at the sound of Emily's voice. Whirling around, I beheld her slender form in the doorway. She sighed and shook her head in mock pity.

"I'm going outside. When you need some help, let me know." She walked away.

I coughed harshly, stumbling after her. "Emily, wait! Please!"

I didn't know where in the house I was. Panic gripped my heart with its icy fingers and began squeezing the life out of me. I was still doing the tripod slide, but it was hard going with one arm because the other was used to cradle Nadalia close. Wicked flames reached out with their long tongues and licked hungrily at my body. The heat made me feel like I was moving in the Tin Man's metal suit, and I struggled with my light burden. I could hear the fire truck's horn resounding through the burning house, sounding like a bullfrog with a bad stomach ache.

"C'mon, you stick in the mud, you!" Emily's soft laugh trickled to me through the smoke.

I saw a flash of red to my right and turned in that direction. Moving through the darkening abyss was never ending. I spotted a small bit of light through the smoke.

That's got to be the way out. But it seems so far away.

Just when it seemed I couldn't inhale smoke one second longer, it literally felt like someone put their hands on my back and shoved me through the doorway. I staggered like a drunk on my knees and rolled onto my back to protect Nadalia from getting crushed. Voices were babbling all around me. Something icy was thrown over my body. It felt heavenly.

Did I die? I wondered.

When my senses returned, I was coughing up a storm. Something covered the lower half of my face as someone called my name repeatedly. My smoke-filled head pounded mercilessly, and my right leg throbbed. I slowly opened my eyes, becoming more aware of my surroundings. A beautiful blue sky was overhead, and I could feel something soft against my bare skin. Two paramedics hovered over me, pressing an oxygen mask over the lower half of my face. My left hand slipped and struck something metallic.

I must be on a gurney.

"He's awake!" Paramedic One shouted.

One of my buddies, Kendrick, came into my field of vision. The officer sighed and shook his head.

"Jay, we know you think you're good-looking, but that was ridiculous."

"Huh?" I grunted, having absolutely *no* idea what he meant.

"You came bursting out of that house with smoke coming off your body like you were hot stuff or something," he said, giving me a grin that showed all twelve of his teeth.

Kendrick and his lame jokes are something I can live without. I grinned weakly in response.

"At least I know what to get you for Christmas." He held up my riot helmet. It was covered with heat blisters and melted in a few spots, including the lower half of the face shield.

I suddenly realized my arms were empty. "Nadalia!" I shouted through the mask.

"Calm down, Hot Stuff. She's over there, alive and receiving treatment." Kendrick pointed to an ambulance sitting on the side of the street.

I managed to crane my neck to spot medics caring for the little girl with her parents close by her side. Their faces were full of elation and pure joy. I knew I should be happy for them, but I couldn't help but feel remorse and a little bit of jealousy. If only I'd been a better husband and rescued my family, that would have been my reaction, and I'd be filled with happiness instead of bitterness and regret.

"Kendrick, you sure the kid's fine?"

"Yeah, she's fine."

I've got to make sure myself. I struggled to stand up.

"Whoa there, John Wayne!" Kendrick put a hand on my shoulder, trying to stop me. "Give yourself a chance to rest before you go gallivanting all over the place. 'Specially with your injured leg."

A white, gauzy bandage covered the right limb, a testament to his remark.

"If you stand on it now, it'll start bleeding again," Paramedic One warned. "Plus, you've got some slight burn marks on your neck. Most likely from falling debris. And your kneecaps are seriously scraped up. I doubt you'll be saying your prayers on your knees anytime soon."

I tried standing again, ignoring the protests of paramedics and Kendrick, and pulled off the oxygen mask. "I'm fine."

Kendrick grunted. "Your funeral."

However, I gripped his arm tightly for several seconds as I got my wobbly legs under control. Thousands of tiny, invisible knives repeatedly shanked my injured limb, but I ignored them. My shirt and jacket were gone, as was the cap, and my once pristine blue pants could be mistaken for a pair of boxer briefs; they were so short.

I limped toward the waiting ambulance while Kendrick stayed behind. I wanted to make sure with my own eyes that Nadalia was okay.

Jeffrey and Alicia were still cooing over their daughter. They stopped their coddling as soon as they caught sight of me. I stood beside the stretcher and looked down at Nadalia. Her eyes were open, revealing them to be the exact color as her mom's. The little girl wiggled her tiny fingers at me.

I waved back. "Hi, Nadalia. Nice to meet you."

With tears streaming down his face once more, Jeffrey grabbed my hand in a hearty handshake. "Thank you!" he choked on the words.

"You saved our precious girl," Alicia added, her soft voice filled with gratitude. She took a step forward, and before I knew it, she gave me the tightest squeeze I'd ever felt a woman give.

She let go and stepped back beside her husband. My throat constricted, and I looked away so I wouldn't make a fool of myself and start blubbing. Instead of crying, I gasped and stumbled backward a step. Jeffrey caught me and must have thought I was still suffering the effects of the smoke because he called Kendrick over.

My heart hammered in my throat as I watched Emily chase Angie through the yard and around the firefighters, floating through the air without ever really touching the ground. Catching our daughter, Emily twirled Angie around. Their laughter floated softly to me on the sluggish summer breeze. Emily caught sight of me and smiled lovingly.

Mouthing the words, "Thank you!" she took Angie's hand, turned, and walked toward the woods.

I watched them go until they vanished. A strange peace settled in my spirit.

I'd been redeemed.

About the Author

Growing up surrounded by storytellers and books, Leah developed a love of reading at an early age. After graduating high school, she pursued an English Literature degree at Jefferson Community College.

She dabbled in writing and was thrilled when her first novel, *The Diamond Caper*, was published. The second book, *Anything But A Diamond*, soon followed. After becoming a mom, she wrote three picture books: *The Day Please Slept In, Something Warm For Grandma,* and *King Robert the Wet. Something Warm for Grandma* won The Written Word Award 2021. Her short story, *The Voice,* was published in The 2023 Writer's Block Anthology.

When she's not writing, she spends time with her family, has her nose in a book, or enjoys a cup of tea.

www.ingramcontent.com/pod-product-compliance
Lightning Source LLC
LaVergne TN
LVHW041645070526
838199LV00053B/3562